D0295384

THE GREATEST ADVENTURES IN THE WORLD

ARTHUR
and the
KING'S
SWORD

TONY BRADMAN & TONY ROSS

ORCHARD BOOKS

LONDON BOROUGH OF SUTTON LIBRARY SERVICE	
02348823 4	
Askews	Dec-2004
JF yF	

ORCHARD BOOKS
96 Leonard Street, London EC2A 4XD
Orchard Books Australia
32/45-51 Huntley Street, Alexandria, NSW 2015
ISBN 1 84362 470 2 (hardback)
ISBN 1 84362 475 3 (paperback)
The text was first published in Great Britain in the form of a gift collection called
Swords, Sorcerers and Superheroes with full colour illustrations by Tony Ross, in 2003
This edition first published in hardback in 2004
First paperback publication in 2005
Text © Tony Bradman 2003
Illustrations © Tony Ross 2004

The rights of Tony Bradman to be identified as the author and of Tony Ross
to be identified as the illustrator of this work have been asserted by them
in accordance with the Copyright, Designs and Patents Act, 1988.

A CIP catalogue record for this book is available from the British Library.
1 3 5 7 9 10 8 6 4 2 (hardback)
1 3 5 7 9 10 8 6 4 2 (paperback)
Printed in Great Britain
www.wattspublishing.co.uk

CONTENTS

CHAPTER ONE

THE MESSENGER

LONG AGO, WHEN BRITAIN WAS
in a dark age of war and famine, a
young boy called Arthur lived far in the
west with his father, Sir Ector, and his big
brother, Kay. Sir Ector was a chieftain,
and they had a fine castle, so they were

safe, and they had plenty
to eat. But Arthur
knew that times
were hard for others.
Kay was nearly a
man, had his own
warhorse, weapons
and armour. Arthur
longed for the day
when he too would
be able to ride a
warhorse like Kay's,
and have a shield
and a great sword
at his side. Kay
knew that, and
loved to tease his little
brother and laugh at him.

Then, one cold and misty winter's morning, a messenger rode into Sir Ector's castle. He said there was to be a great meeting of Britain's warlords and chieftains, and that Sir Ector was invited to come. Sir Ector said he would be there, so the messenger galloped off to spread his news elsewhere.

"I hope you'll be taking me with you,
Father," said an excited Kay.

"Yes, of course," said Sir Ector. "You'd
better come too, Arthur."

Arthur hadn't expected that, so he was
surprised and very pleased.

"But why, Father?" said Kay. "He's a boy,
and this is man's work!"

"He'll be a man soon enough," Sir Ector said, glancing at Arthur, "and this will help him learn what that means. Besides, you'll need a squire, Kay."

As Kay's squire, Arthur would have to look after his brother's weapons and armour, but he didn't mind that. And Kay seemed to like the idea of being able to give his brother orders, so he didn't complain any more.

A week later, Sir Ector rode off with Kay, Arthur and a small band of warriors. The meeting was to be held in London, the old Roman capital on the opposite side of the country, and a long journey lay ahead of them.

CHAPTER TWO

THE GREAT UTHER PENDRAGON

ARTHUR HAD NEVER BEEN away from home before. At first he was as excited as Kay, both of them eager to see new sights. But the further they travelled east, the worse things looked. They passed through burnt fields and villages and towns, and wherever they went the people were hungry and scared.

"This is awful, Father," Arthur said eventually. Kay was riding with the warriors, but Arthur was beside Sir Ector. Arthur was very upset by what he was seeing. It was like riding through some kind of terrible nightmare, he thought. "I don't understand," he said. "Why are things so bad everywhere?"

"It started when the Romans left us to defend ourselves," Sir Ector said quietly, his face grim. "The Saxons invaded, and they've been spreading from the east like a plague ever since, killing our people and taking the land. And the warlords make it worse by squabbling and fighting with each other."

"Why don't they join together to fight the Saxons?" said Arthur.

"Because none of them trust any of the others," said Sir Ector. "And no one has been strong enough to make them listen to reason, not since the days of the last king, the great Uther Pendragon. But even he couldn't keep them under his control for long enough to sweep the Saxons from our shores."

"What happened to him, Father?" Arthur asked. "Did he die in battle?"

"No, Arthur," said Sir Ector quietly, turning towards him as he spoke. Arthur could see Sir Ector had a strange look on his face. "It's thought that some of the warlords plotted against him, and that he was poisoned along with all his family. But nobody has ever really known the whole truth..."

They rode in silence after that, Arthur thinking deeply. He wished that he could do something to help. But what power did he have? He was only a boy, still too young to achieve anything in the hard world of men and war.

"So who has called this meeting, Father?" Arthur asked after a while.

"I don't know," said Sir Ector. "But I do know this might well be our last chance to save ourselves. Although I doubt that the warlords will agree…"

Then Kay came riding up, and Arthur asked no more questions.

CHAPTER THREE

THE HOODED FIGURE

A FEW DAYS LATER THEY arrived at the gates of London, and entered the city. Most of the old Roman buildings were ruined, and the streets were crowded with hard, tough men – the warlords of Britain and their

17

followers – their eyes cold, their faces scarred from battle. Distrust hung over the city like a fog.

"Wait here while we find out what's happening, Arthur," said Sir Ector.

Then Sir Ector strode off with his warriors and Kay, leaving Arthur to guard the horses. Arthur noticed Kay's sword hanging from his saddle.

Suddenly Arthur was distracted from his watching by the sound of loud, angry voices. He left the horses to see what was going on, and a tall, dark figure in a hooded cloak brushed by him as he did so, seeming almost to glide over the cobbles like a ghost. Arthur stopped and shivered, the little hairs on the back of his neck standing on end as he watched the figure slip away. Then he shook his head to clear it, and carried on in the same direction he'd been going in before.

Two warriors had been arguing, but by the time Arthur reached them, they had settled their differences and moved off. Arthur quickly returned to the horses, suddenly feeling worried. One look told him Kay's sword wasn't hanging from his saddle any more. Just then Kay himself appeared, alone. "Father sent me back for my sword," Kay said. "Where is it?"

"I don't know…" Arthur said. "I…I think it's been stolen."

"Well, it's your fault," Kay snarled at him. "You're my squire, and you were supposed to be looking after it! So you'd better find me another sword – and be quick about it, or I'll have to tell Father just how useless you are."

Arthur ran from his brother. Night was falling, and Arthur wandered the gloomy, ruined streets of London. Men were clustering for warmth now round their campfires. Arthur wondered how he could have been so stupid – and where he could possibly find another sword to replace the one that he had lost.

Then he bumped into that tall, dark, hooded figure for a second time.

"You may find what you seek in there," said the hooded man, and pointed beyond him. Arthur looked, and saw a large pavilion in a nearby courtyard.

When he turned round again, the hooded man had vanished into the darkness! It seemed even stranger than before, but though the hairs on the back of his neck stood up again, Arthur didn't stop to think about it.

He slipped into the pavilion. It contained a block of stone surrounded by tall candles that cast a golden glow. There was some writing carved on the stone, which Arthur ignored. He was too busy looking at the sword sticking into it. Arthur grabbed the hilt and pulled, and the sword came out smoothly. A tingle shot up his arm, but Arthur ignored that too, and went to find Kay.

"Now that's what I call a sword," said
Kay, grabbing it without thanks.

Arthur hadn't noticed quite how
good a sword it was, with its jewelled
pommel and its fine steel blade that
seemed to catch the light at every turn.

But when the boys found their father, Sir
Ector noticed the sword immediately.

"That's not your sword, Kay," he said.
Sir Ector wanted to know what had
happened to Kay's own sword, and where
he'd got the other.

Kay blustered, claiming he'd swapped his old sword for the new one. Sir Ector obviously didn't believe a word of it, and Arthur finally told their father the truth.

"Take me to this stone, Arthur," said Sir Ector. "I want to see it."

Arthur did as he was ordered.

CHAPTER FOUR

THE SWORD

THE THREE OF THEM WENT through the dark streets to the courtyard, and the pavilion was the same as when Arthur had left it, the block of stone standing inside, the candles still burning, no one else there. But now Sir

Ector stood in front of it and read the carved writing aloud. "He who draws the sword from the stone is the true-born King of Britain."

"Arthur was lying, Father," said Kay, quickly stepping forward. "He didn't pull the sword from the stone – it was me! So I must be the true-born king."

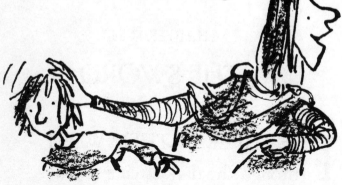

"Well then, it should be easy for you to perform this miracle once more, my son," said Sir Ector. "Put the sword back in the stone and pull it out."

Kay placed the tip of the sword on the stone, and it slid in up to the hilt with a clang. Then Kay pulled…and nothing happened.

He pulled till his face was red and he groaned, but the sword wouldn't move. Then Sir Ector tried, using all his strength, and still the sword stayed stuck in the stone.

31

"Now you try, Arthur," Sir Ector said at last.

Arthur gripped the hilt in a daze, gave the gentlest of tugs – and the sword came out smoothly. Arthur felt that tingle in his arm again, but far more powerfully. He stared at the sword, spellbound by its beauty. Then he saw that his father and brother were kneeling before him, their heads bowed.

"But why are you kneeling before me?" Arthur said. "I…I can't be king…"

"Ah, but you can, Arthur," said a loud voice. "The proof is in your hand.

You are the true-born son of a king, and you will be King of the Britons."

Arthur looked round and saw that tall, hooded figure for a third time. The man threw back his hood to reveal a face that was both old and young, his eyes a deep, forest green, his white hair swept off his high, pale forehead.

"Merlin!" said Sir Ector. "I should have known you were behind all this."

Arthur had heard tales of the legendary Merlin, although till that moment he had never suspected the wizard might actually be real.

Arthur, however, was more interested in what Merlin had said than in the wizard's fame.

"But Sir Ector is my father," Arthur said. "And he isn't a king."

"I have always loved you as my son, Arthur," said Sir Ector. "But you are not of my blood.

Your real father was the great Uther Pendragon himself…"Arthur listened in utter amazement as Sir Ector told the story. Uther had known of the warlords' plot against him, and had asked Merlin to save his baby son. So one dark, windswept night, Merlin had spirited Arthur away to Sir Ector's castle. Sir Ector had already agreed to bring up Arthur as his own son, and had never told anyone that Uther Pendragon was Arthur's true father.

"I thank you from the bottom of my heart," Arthur said at last. He was deeply moved at the thought of what Sir Ector had done for him. "And I swear that whatever happens in the future, I will always think of you as my father. And you, Kay, will always be my brother – if that is your wish too."

Kay smiled at him and said it was, and

the three of them joined hands.

"I've long kept watch over you, Arthur," said Merlin, "and the time has come for you to take your rightful place. It was I who called the warlords and chieftains together – so you could show yourself to them as their king. We need a leader, someone who can unite us against the Saxons once more."

"But I'm too young," said Arthur,
self-doubt and fear suddenly filling his
heart. "Men like that will never accept
me as their leader…will they?"

Merlin just smiled, and told him to put
the sword back in the stone.

The next morning, Merlin summoned all the warlords and the chieftains to the courtyard. The pavilion had been taken down in the night, and the sword in the stone was there for all to see. An excited murmur ran through them as they read the writing. Arthur stood behind the crowd with Sir Ector and Kay.

"Behold the test of kingship!" said Merlin. "Each man shall try his hand."

And one by one, the warlords and chieftains did try, but with no success. No matter how they strained, none could pull the sword from the stone.

Then Merlin called for Arthur, and

the youth stepped forward and slowly
made his way through the crowd. The
warlords and chieftains stared at him and
muttered suspiciously. Arthur gripped
the hilt, and they gasped as he pulled
the sword free of the stone, that tingle
shooting up his arm again.

Arthur raised the sword on high – but now the crowd was angry.

"It's a trick!" somebody yelled. "Kill the wizard... and the boy!" Several warriors drew their swords and advanced. And suddenly Arthur realised he was not afraid. He had been waiting for this moment his whole life. He knew what to do, and that he would also know what to do when it came to fighting the Saxons and saving his people from fear and hunger.

Arthur leapt into action, his blade flashing in the morning sunlight as he parried the warriors' savage blows with unbelievable speed and skill, the clang of steel on steel filling the air. He fought like a man, like the king they needed to lead them. And soon he had those fierce warriors at his mercy…

The tingle now filled him from head to foot. Power flashed from his eyes.

"Kneel to your king, Britons!" roared Merlin, and the crowd obeyed.

The legend of King Arthur had begun.

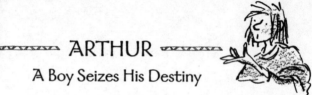

ARTHUR
A Boy Seizes His Destiny

By Tony Bradman

The legend of King Arthur is known all over the world, and there have been countless books, plays and films about him. But did he really exist? Some historians think he might have been a fifth century Celtic chieftain, fighting the invading Saxons after the Romans abandoned Britain. Stories about him appeared in several books in the early middle ages, most famously in the twelfth century *History of the Kings of Britain* by Geoffrey of Monmouth.

Arthur's legend grew through the centuries, acquiring all sorts of magical elements and characters. Everyone's heard of Camelot, the Knights of the Round Table, Arthur's wife Guinevere and the wizard Merlin. By the nineteenth century, the legend was no longer simply the tale of a chieftain fighting for his people, but a great cycle of poetic stories full of fantasy and romance.

Arthur has always been a hero, of course, and that's why we're attracted to him and want to experience his stories. He's strong, noble and generous and he wins battles – although in the later stories he does come to a tragic end. But that's part of his appeal too. Arthur is a character with a destiny.

People all over the world have always been fascinated by the idea that our lives might be destined to turn out a certain way, that Fate lies in wait for us whatever we do. It runs through Greek mythology – there's a strong feeling in the stories of characters such as Jason and Theseus that whatever else they do, their fates are mapped out for them. In the tale of William Tell, a legendary Swiss hero, he tries to avoid being drawn into the struggle against the occupying Austrians. But there's no escape. And one way or another, we know he's bound to fight them.

At the beginning of this story, Arthur might be just a boy, but he's the only one who can pull the sword from the stone, whether he likes it or not. In seizing the sword he seizes his destiny – and from that moment on we want to go with him and find out what it is!

ORCHARD MYTHS AND CLASSICS

THE GREATEST ADVENTURES IN THE WORLD

TONY BRADMAN & TONY ROSS

Ali Baba and the Stolen Treasure	1 84362 473 7
Jason and the Voyage to the Edge of the World	1 84362 472 9
Robin Hood and the Silver Arrow	1 84362 474 5
Aladdin and the Fabulous Genie	1 84362 477 X
Arthur and the King's Sword	1 84362 475 3
William Tell and the Apple for Freedom	1 84362 476 1

All priced at £3.99

Orchard Black Apples are available from all good bookshops, or can be ordered
direct from the publisher: Orchard Books, PO BOX 29, Douglas IM99 1BQ
Credit card orders please telephone 01624 836000
or fax 01624 837033or visit our Internet site: www.wattspub.co.uk
or e-mail: bookshop@enterprise.net for details.

To order please quote title, author and ISBN
and your full name and address.
Cheques and postal orders should be made payable to 'Bookpost plc.'
Postage and packing is FREE within the UK
(overseas customers should add £1.00 per book).

Prices and availability are subject to change.